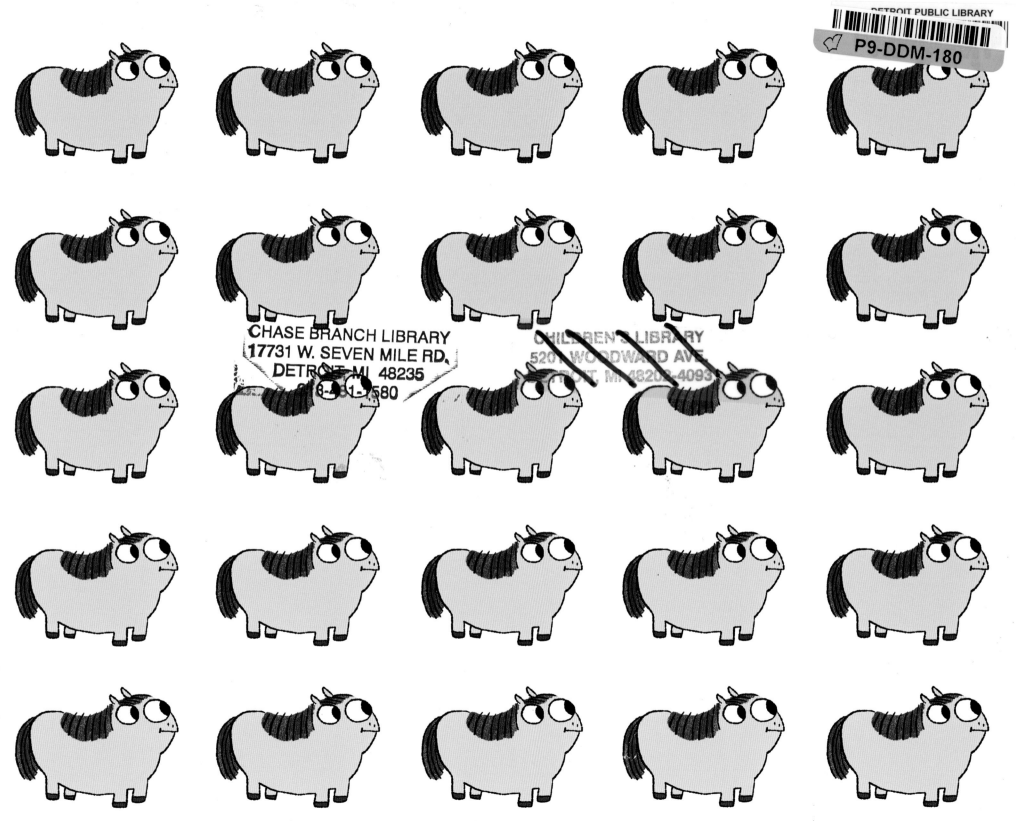

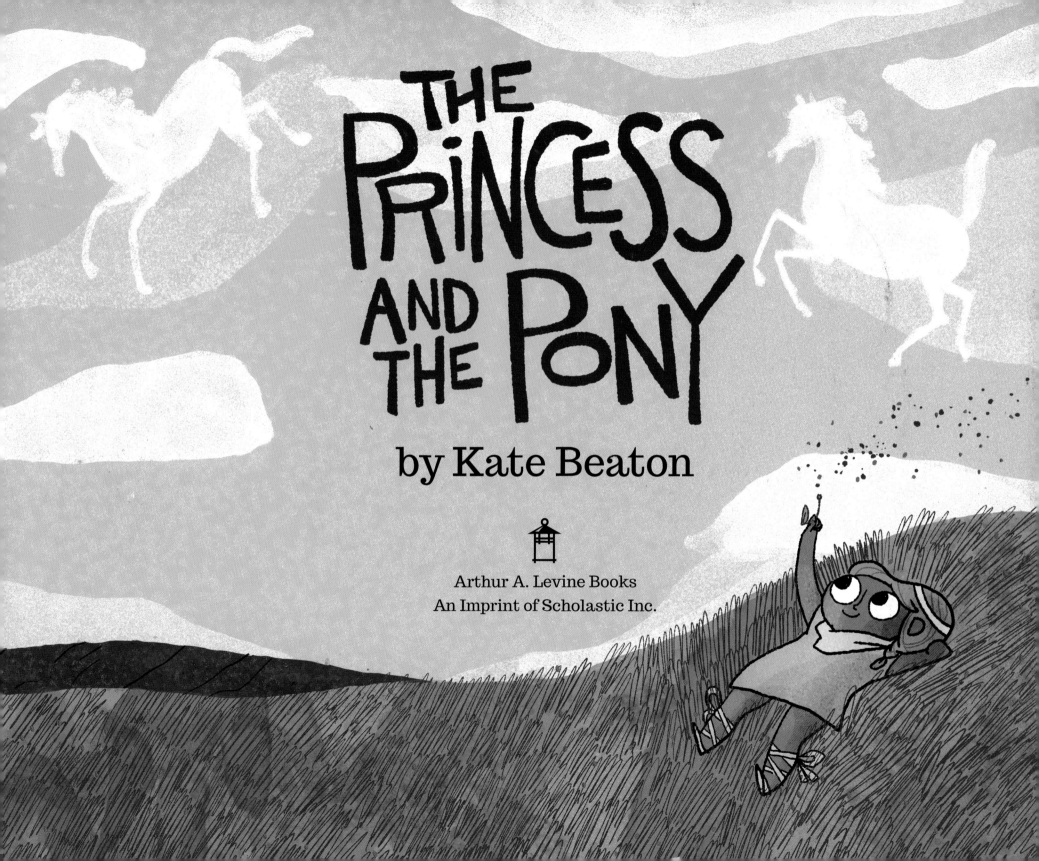

THE PRINCESS AND THE PONY

by Kate Beaton

Arthur A. Levine Books
An Imprint of Scholastic Inc.

LIBRARY OF CONGRESS CATALOGING-IN-PUBLICATION DATA
Beaton, Kate, 1983- author, illustrator.
The princess and the pony / Kate Beaton. First edition.   pages cm
Summary: Princess Pinecone would like a real war horse for her birthday, instead of which she gets a plump,
cute pony—but sometimes cuteness can be a kind of weapon, especially in a fight with dodgeballs and spitballs
and hairballs and squareballs. ISBN 978-0-545-63708-4 (hardcover : alk. paper) 1. Ponies—Juvenile fiction.
2. Princesses—Juvenile fiction. [1. Ponies—Fiction. 2. Princesses—Fiction. 3. Humorous stories.] I. Title.
PZ7.1.B434Pr 2015   [E]—dc23   2014030927

10 9 8 7 6 5 4   16 17 18 19
Printed in Malaysia   108
First edition, July 2015

The art for this book was created digitally.
Book design by Kate Beaton and David Saylor

For my sisters, Becky, Maura, and Laureen

In a kingdom of warriors,

the smallest warrior was Princess Pinecone.
And she was very excited for her birthday.

Most warriors get fantastic birthday presents. Shields, amulets,
helmets with horns on them. Things to win battles with.
Things that make them feel like champions.

Princess Pinecone got a lot of cozy sweaters.
Warriors do not need cozy sweaters.

This year, it would be different. Pinecone made sure to let everyone
know exactly what she wanted: A big horse. A fast horse.
A strong horse. A real warrior's horse!

And they tried their best . . .

But they didn't get it quite right.

"I can't ride that!"
said Princess Pinecone.

"It's too small!"
"It's too round!"

"And I think its eyes are
looking in different directions . . ."
(This was true, but only sometimes.)

But you can't say no to a birthday present, so she took the little pony to her room, where it ate things it shouldn't have, and farted too much.

Now, as it happens, a great battle was coming up,
and battling is a warrior's favorite thing to do.

The princess tried to teach the pony
how to be a real warrior horse . . .

. . . but the pony was hopeless.
"We'll never be champions," Pinecone sighed.

The day of the great battle arrived.
All the other warriors seemed very big and very tough.
"Just . . . do your best," she told the pony.

The starting horn sounded, and what a battle it was!
There were dodgeballs and spitballs and hairballs
and squareballs (those were new).

People were getting knocked over left and right.
Pinecone stood at the edge, looking for her chance to dive in.

Just then, Otto the Awful, the meanest warrior of all, charged right for her!

The crowd held its breath.
Pinecone fumbled for her spitballs . . .

. . . but Otto stopped in his tracks.
His eyes grew very wide.

"Awww," he said, "what a cute little pony!
Who would want to hurt a roly-poly pony like you?"

Warrior after warrior paused to admire the pony.
"What a cutie pie!" said Sally Smash. "He's so round!" said Carlos the Cruel.
"Aww, he looks a bit like me!" said Huge Harald.

Pinecone was flabbergasted, flummoxed, floored!
"This is not how a battle usually goes," she said.

"You're right," said Otto.
"But we warriors don't often get to show our cuddly sides."

Princess Pinecone thought about it.
"Well," she said, "I can help you with that."

Soon all the warriors had their own cozy sweaters!

They were looking pretty cuddly, for a bunch of brutes.

Everyone voted Pinecone and the pony the Most Valuable Warriors of the day.

Pinecone threw her arms around the pony.
"You're the best horse a warrior could ask for!" she cheered.
"Nothing can stop a team like us!"

The little pony was so excited, it lifted its tail and farted.

"Well," said Pinecone, "we can work on that."

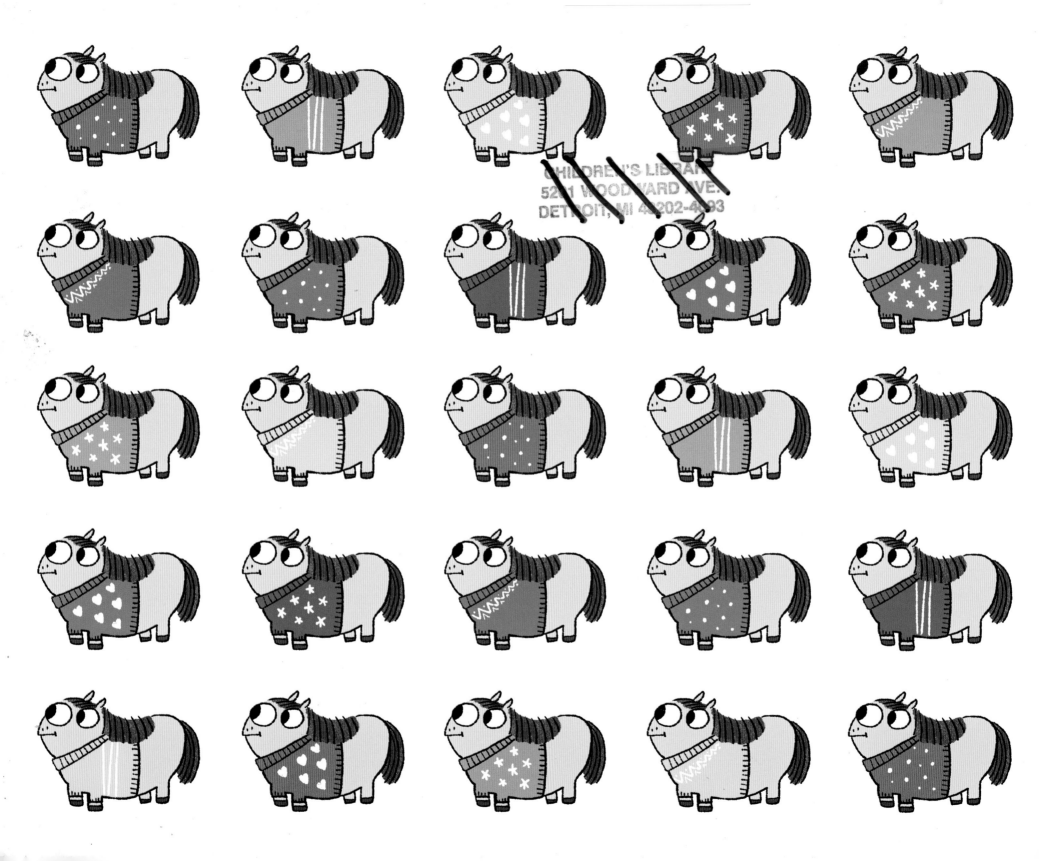